THE LONELY LIONESS
and the Ostrich Chicks

A MASAI TALE

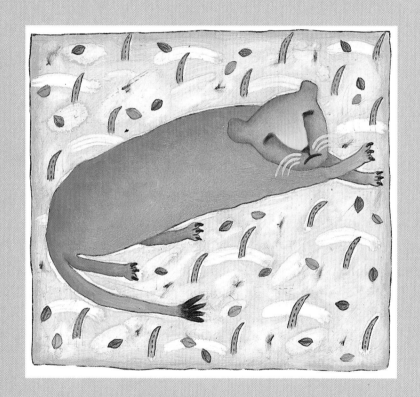

Retold by Verna Aardema · Illustrated by Yumi Heo

Alfred A. Knopf • New York

To my grandson, Jim Aardema

—V. A.

To my wonderful husband, Steven

—Y. H.

The Lonely Lioness and the Ostrich Chicks is retold from a tale in Verna Aardema's book *Tales for the Third Ear,* published by E. P. Dutton, New York, 1969. That book is out of print, and the rights have been returned to Mrs. Aardema.

The previous source was "The Story of the Ostrich Chicks," in *The Masai: Their Language and Folklore,* by Claude Hollis, published by Oxford University Press, London, 1905.

THIS IS A BORZOI BOOK PUBLISHED BY ALFRED A. KNOPF, INC.
Text copyright © 1996 by Verna Aardema
Illustrations copyright © 1996 by Yumi Heo

Library of Congress Cataloging-in-Publication Data

Aardema, Verna.
The lonely lioness and the ostrich chicks: a Masai tale / retold by Verna Aardema ; illustrations by Yumi Heo.
p.   cm.
Summary: In this retelling of a Masai tale, a mongoose helps an ostrich get her chicks back from the lonely lioness who has stolen them.
ISBN 0-679-86934-4 (trade) — ISBN 0-679-96934-9 (lib. bdg.)
[1. Masai (African people)—Folklore. 2. Folklore—Africa.] I. Heo, Yumi, ill. II. Title.
PZ8.1.A213Lo   1996   398.2—dc20   94-48449   [E]

Printed in the United States of America
10 9 8 7 6 5 4 3 2 1

http://www.randomhouse.com/

Even the ostrich, with its long neck and sharp eyes, cannot see what will happen in the future.

—Masai proverb

One day, a mother ostrich—unaware of danger lurking ahead—led her newly hatched chicks to feed under a tree in which a lioness was sleeping.

The chattering of the mother and the cheeping of the chicks woke up the lioness. She looked down at the ostriches as they searched for seeds and bugs in the grass. And she said to herself, "What a beautiful family Mother Ostrich has! *Four* chicks! I would be happy to have just *one* child."

As she watched the ostriches, the lioness got an idea—she would catch one of the chicks. Then she would no longer be lonely.

Presently, a grasshopper whirred past Mother Ostrich, and she turned aside to chase it. At once, the lioness leaped down, *gurum!* right between the mother bird and her babies.

The frightened chicks ran, *pamdal*, in every direction. But the lioness quickly gathered them together and began to comfort them. She was pleased to have all four, instead of only one. She licked their heads, and from deep in her throat she purred, *irtil-irtil-irtil*.

The lioness was so kind to the chicks that they soon forgot she was not their mother. And when she set out for her den, they followed in a line behind her.

Mother Ostrich saw what was happening. "Don't steal my chicks!" she screamed.

"They are not yours anymore," replied the lioness. "They belong to me now." And she hurried on, with the chicks struggling to keep up.

Mother Ostrich came stamping, *gum, gum, gum,* after the lioness, pleading, "Give me back my chicks! Give me back my chicks!"

The lioness ignored her. So Mother Ostrich ran to her and begged, "Please don't eat them! Promise you won't eat them!"

"Of course I won't eat them," said Lioness. "Does a mother eat her own children?"

"*Ssss,*" hissed Mother Ostrich.

Just then a gazelle came along.

Mother Ostrich called, "Oh, Gazelle, will you help me? Lioness is stealing my chicks and calling them her children!"

The gazelle answered, "I wouldn't argue with a lioness if she said that the moon was her cub." And he went bounding away, *yir-id-de, yir-id-de, yir-id-de.*

The lioness hastened on with her new babies. And Mother Ostrich stamped along behind them, crying, "Give me back my chicks! Give me back my chicks!"

Soon the little procession met a hyena. Mother Ostrich called, "Oh, Hyena, will you help me? Lioness is stealing my chicks and calling them her children!"

"Well," said the cowardly hyena. "The babies are following the lioness. Babies follow their mothers. So they must belong to her." And he slunk away, *pasa, pasa, pasa.*

"*Nnnn,*" groaned Mother Ostrich. Then, flapping her wings to help her go faster, she raced to catch up to the lioness, shouting, "Give me back my chicks! Give me back my chicks!"

Soon they met a jackal. Mother Ostrich called, "Oh, Jackal, will you help me? Lioness is stealing my chicks and calling them her children."

"I will try," said the jackal.

He looked sideways at the lioness. Then he asked cautiously, "Excuse me, gentle Lioness. If those little creatures are your children, shouldn't they have four feet?"

"They *do* have four feet," snapped Lioness. "Their front feet are just beginning to grow." And she pointed to a little wing on the nearest chick.

The lioness went right on past the jackal, with the ostriches following her, and Mother Ostrich screaming, "Give me back my chicks! Give me back my chicks!"

Farther along, they came upon a mongoose burrow. The animal was sunning himself beside the entrance.

Mother Ostrich said, "Oh, Mongoose, will you help me? Lioness is stealing my chicks and calling them her children."

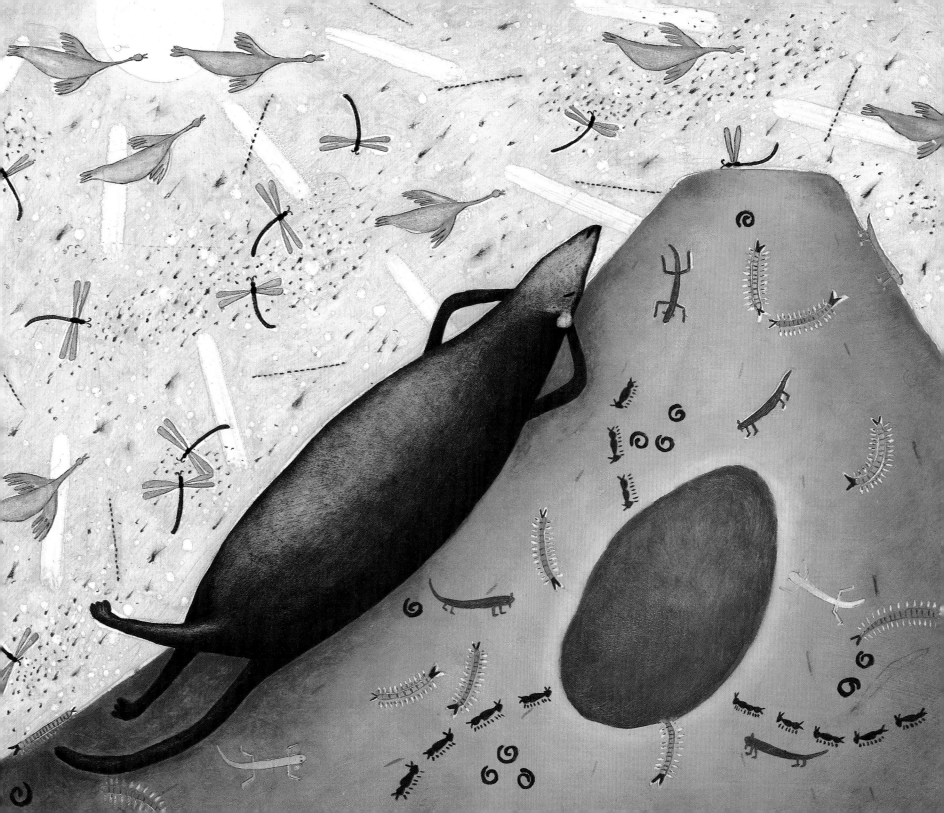

Now, the mongoose may be small, but he is fearless—he kills and eats poisonous snakes! He nodded to Mother Ostrich as if to say, *I'll do it*. Then he turned to the lioness and taunted, "Lioness, you are a bigger fool than I thought you were!"

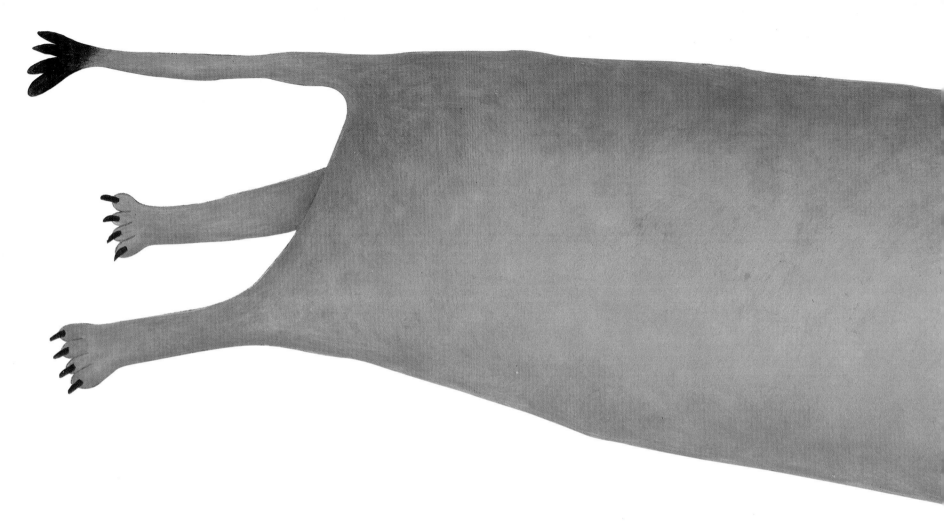

"AH-ROOAH!" roared the lioness as she sprang at him.
But the mongoose was too quick. He had already skedaddled,
dik-dak-dilak, into his burrow.

The lioness peered in but could see nothing. So she crouched beside the opening, and waited...and waited...and waited for the mongoose to come out.

And while she waited, Mother Ostrich quietly rounded up her chicks and walked them home, *tuk-pik, tuk-pik, tuk-pik.*